THE FERNS WAVED BACK

Barbara Davidson

illustrated by Kerrie Robertson

The Ferns Waved Back

First Edition

Hardcover ISBN: 978-1-63837-400-8
Paperback ISBN: 978-1-63837-401-5
eBook ISBN: 978-1-63837-402-2

lovingly dedicated
to my sweet grandson
greyson and all of my
nature loving friends

It was a beautiful spring morning as Greyson and his Grandma began their walk through the forest that surrounded their backyard. The sun's rays reflected off Greyson's face like a little flashlight, shining the way to an exciting adventure ahead! Racing across the moist grass, his blond hair dancing and swirling around his face, Greyson squealed with excitement. Chipmunks, squirrels and squawking blue jays scampered and flapped all around, drawing them into the woods, as if leading them in a parade.

In the forest, the shade from the tall trees began to block out the sun above. Below, there was a carpet of pine needles that lined the pathway. As they crunched their feet over them, there was a sweet aroma in the air. Greyson took a deep breath, "it smells like Christmas!" He ran ahead of Grandma, swinging his arms back and forth like a little baby bird trying to fly. "Wait up little one," called Grandma. Greyson found a large, oval-shaped rock covered with moss and jumped up on it to wait for his Grandma. "Look at me," he yelled, "I am king of the forest!" His grandmother caught up to him and grinned, "you certainly are my boy." Greyson proudly leapt down, and they continued on their journey.

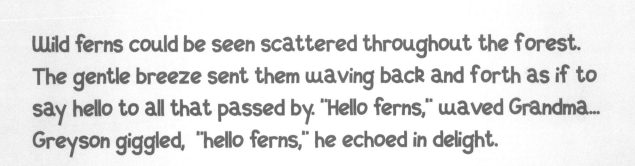

Wild ferns could be seen scattered throughout the forest. The gentle breeze sent them waving back and forth as if to say hello to all that passed by. "Hello ferns," waved Grandma... Greyson giggled, "hello ferns," he echoed in delight.

"Wow Grandma, look at that," gasped Greyson, pointing to a long-fallen tree. Grandma smiled. "Oh that's nature's balance beam, hop on and walk along it." Greyson jumped up and began to walk along the fallen tree. He was a bit wobbly at first but soon got his balance. Pretending to be a gymnast, he placed one foot in front of the other all along the tree's trunk. After going back and forth a few times, Greyson hopped off and continued down the trail.

The light coming through the trees cast a bright white line down their path. Greyson began to hop over it, as if playing a game of hopscotch. Grandma called out, "one-two-three-hop,four-five-six-stop." Grandma was always making up games and rhyming songs. Greyson loved that!

All of a sudden, they heard a sound like someone knocking at the door. "That's a woodpecker," said Grandma, "lets go see if we can find him." They began looking all around the trees, walking closer and closer toward the sound until Greyson spotted the woodpecker halfway up a pine tree. "Why is he knocking so loudly on the tree?" asked Greyson. "He is using his bill to tap on the tree to see if it has any insects inside to eat," answered Grandma. They decided to sit on a stump of a tree and have a snack, while enjoying the woodpecker's performance.

"Hey, something is tickling my leg," cried Greyson! Grandma observed that there was a tiny spider crawling along the side of his leg. She gently scooped it off and onto the forest floor. As she did, her eye caught a magnificently shaped spider's web, glistening in the sun's rays. "I think I found the spider's home," announced Grandma. She explained that this silky web was made by the spider to help catch bugs for the spider to eat. "So spiders and woodpeckers both like to eat bugs," thought Greyson. He sprang up and ran over to the web. "It's so beautiful," he gasped, "can we put the spider back in its web?" "The spider will find its way on his own," she reassured him.

"Speaking of finding your way, we should begin to find our own way home too." Grandma and Greyson held hands as they ventured back down the trail, enjoying the sights, sounds and smells of the forest. The shade the trees provided kept them nice and cool, with the glimpses of sunlight through the trees like a gentle warm hug. They balanced their way back down the fallen tree, waved goodbye to the ferns and stepped around the moss-covered rock, merrily heading home.

the end

ABOUT THE AUTHOR:

Barbara Davidson lives on the eastern shores of
Lake Ontario with her husband Dwight and their
sweet dog, Rumi. Her greatest writing inspirations
come from her two children, Sara and Alex
and her adorable grandson ,Greyson.